PUFFIN BOOKS

Bear's Bad Mood

Bear's Bad Mood

Written and illustrated by
John Prater

PUFFIN BOOKS

PUFFIN BOOKS

Published by the Penguin Group
Penguin Books Ltd, 27 Wrights Lane, London W8 5TZ, England
Penguin Putnam Inc., 375 Hudson Street, New York, New York 10014, USA
Penguin Books Australia Ltd, Ringwood, Victoria, Australia
Penguin Books Canada Ltd, 10 Alcorn Avenue, Toronto, Ontario, Canada M4V 3B2
Penguin Books (NZ) Ltd, Private Bag 102902, NSMC, Auckland, New Zealand

Penguin Books Ltd, Registered Offices: Harmondsworth, Middlesex, England

First published by Hamish Hamilton Ltd 1990
Published in Puffin Books 1997
5 7 9 10 6

The moral right of the author and illustrator has been asserted

Filmset in Plantin

Printed in Hong Kong by Midas Printing Limited

It was like any other day in Bear's home.
Mum was singing along with the radio.
Dad was noisily washing up the dishes.
He made lots of bubbles as he clattered
the pans around.

Bear's two little sisters were in the
living room. They were arguing about
who had made all the mess.

Everything was just the same as usual.
Except for Bear.

He was lying on his bed, feeling very cross. He wasn't sure why exactly. He just didn't feel like doing anything at all today.

It had all started when Dad had come
into his room early that morning. He was
pretending to be an alarm clock and was
banging a pan with a spoon and
shouting, "Wakey-wakey!"

Dad thought it was a really funny joke,
but Bear didn't.

Then Bear fell over the train set his sister had left next to his bed and he banged his elbow.

At breakfast the Yummy Honey cereal packet was empty and he had to have lumpy porridge instead.

Finally, Mum told him that he would have to take his sisters to the park that afternoon while she and Dad went shopping.

"I'm fed up!" groaned Bear, going back to bed and pulling the duvet over his head.

Suddenly the door flew open and his
sisters burst in. They were hitting each
other with pillows and feathers were
flying everywhere.

"Go away!" yelled Bear. "GO AWAY!"

"What's going on?" said Mum, coming
into the room. "Just look at this mess. Go
outside, all of you."

Bear wandered miserably into the garden. His heart sank when he saw his friends were already there.

They came running over to him.

"Hello Bear," said Fox.

"What shall we play today?" asked Dog.

"Let's have a race on our bikes," suggested Mole.

"No, I don't want to," said Bear
grumpily. "I'm not in the mood."

Bear turned away and strode off down
the path.

His friends stared after him in surprise.
This wasn't like Bear. He was usually the
first to suggest a game.

Bear had now disappeared round the
corner of the house. The others set off
after him.

Bear looked behind him and decided to
hide in the shed.

He could hear his friends laughing and chattering as he climbed inside a large trunk and pulled down the lid.

"They won't find me now," he thought.

Moments later the lid was raised and a big wet nose touched Bear's cheek.

"You can't hide from me!" said Dog. "I can smell you easily."

Bear jumped out of the trunk. He surprised his friends by running straight for the door and slamming it behind him.

He ran down the path, dived through a
flower bush and hid in the vegetable
patch. Pulling an onion out of the ground,
he rubbed it all over himself.

"That will fool them," he thought.
"They'll *never* smell me now."
Sitting very still, he closed his eyes.

Suddenly he felt hot breath in his ear and he opened his eyes to find Fox grinning at him.

"I could hear you breathing," said Fox.

"Oh NO!" shouted Bear, as he burst out of the bushes and ran across to the oak tree.

The twisted roots of the tree held a den
where they all played. It was a maze of
tunnels which Bear knew better than
anyone. He squeezed through a small gap
and was then deep under the tree, where
the light was dim.

"It's a bit damp," thought Bear, "but
they won't find me here."

Just then the ground beneath him started wriggling and Bear found himself moving upwards.

As he banged his head on the roof of the den, a twitching nose appeared between his feet.

"Hello," said Mole. "I knew you were here. I could feel your heart beating right through the ground."

Bear was running out of hiding places. He wriggled out of the tree and ran back to the house.

"I'll disguise myself so no one will recognise me," he thought.

He ran into his sisters' room.

"These are just what I need," growled Bear.

Bear crept outside in his disguise and sat on the swing. Everything was quiet. Then he heard muffled snorts and giggles behind him. He turned round to see his friends rolling about with laughter.

"You do look silly, Bear!" they howled.

"Right," snarled Bear, throwing off his hat and glasses. "Perhaps I can't hide from you, but I CAN go somewhere you can't follow."

He began climbing the giant oak tree.

Bear was quite right. No one else could climb like him. He clambered upwards until he was swaying in the warm breeze amongst the highest branches.

Far below, his friends looked up until their necks ached, and Bear looked happily down at them.

"At last," sighed Bear, shutting his eyes, "there is no one to annoy me."

But now Bear had forgotten why he wanted to get away from his friends in the first place! In fact, he'd been so busy running and hiding that he couldn't remember the reason for his bad mood.

"I think I might go and play after all," he decided.

Bear opened his eyes and found it was no longer bright and sunny. A huge dark cloud loomed over the tree and the breeze was quickly becoming a gusty wind.

"OOH!" thought Bear. "I'd better climb down."

But the whole tree was swaying back and forth with such force that Bear could not reach the branch below him.

Plop! A large drop of water fell on his nose as the first drops of rain pattered down.

A few seconds later, Bear was soaked to the skin. He felt very frightened as he dangled helplessly in the storm.

CRAASH! A sudden flash of lightning and the boom of thunder startled Bear. He lost his grip on the branch and began to slither and tumble down the tree towards the ground.

"HELP!" he yelled.

A great, furry paw grabbed him as he fell.

Bear found himself cradled in Dad's arms.

Bear's friends had fetched his dad when
they saw he was stuck in the tree. Dad
had climbed halfway up the tree and
caught Bear as he fell.

"Silly boy!" said Dad, as they
clambered down. "What were you doing
up the tree anyway?"

Bear's friends were sheltering at the
base of the tree, looking worried.

"Gosh, Bear, I'm glad you are safe,"
said Mole.

"We'll see you again soon, then. 'Bye,"
said Dog.

"Hey, where are you going?" said
Bear, as his friends started to leave.

"Well, you don't want to play, do
you?" replied Fox.

"Yes . . . no . . . that is, I didn't, but I do
now," muttered Bear.

"I think he was just in a bad mood,"
said Dad with a smile.

"Well, I'm not any more," said Bear.
"Anyway, look, the sun's coming out."

The storm had passed over now and the rain had stopped.

"Let's go roller-skating!" yelled Bear.

And Bear and his friends played happily – and it had never felt better.

Also available in First Young Puffin

WHAT STELLA SAW
Wendy Smith

Stella's mum is a fortune-teller who always gets things wrong. But when football-mad Stella starts reading tea leaves, she seems to be right every time! Or is she . . .

THE DAY THE SMELLS WENT WRONG
Catherine Sefton

It is just an ordinary day, but Jackie and Phil can't understand why nothing smells as it should. Toast smells like tar, fruit smells like fish, and their school dinners smell of perfume! Together, Jackie and Phil discover the cause of the problem . . .

BELLA AT THE BALLET
Brian Ball

Bella has been looking forward to her first ballet lesson for ages – but she's cross when Mum says Baby Tommy is coming with them. Bella is sure Tommy will spoil everything, but in the end it's hard to know who enjoys the class more – Bella or Tommy!